Jazz and Jet

Written by Kate Scott

Illustrated by Elena Selivanova

Collins

This is Jazz.

This is Jet.

Jet zigs and zags.

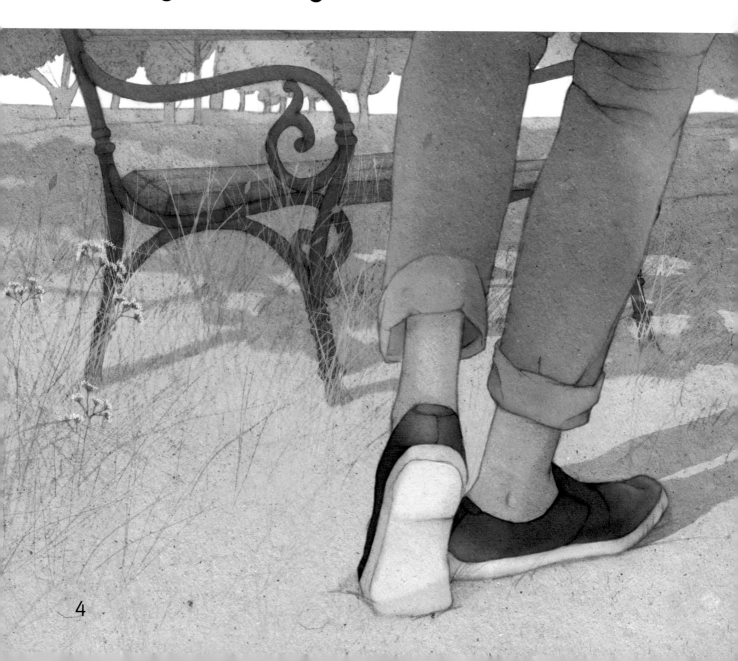

Jazz is in bed.

Quick, Jazz, run!

Jet gets wet by the shed.

Jet gets in.

Jet has a chill.

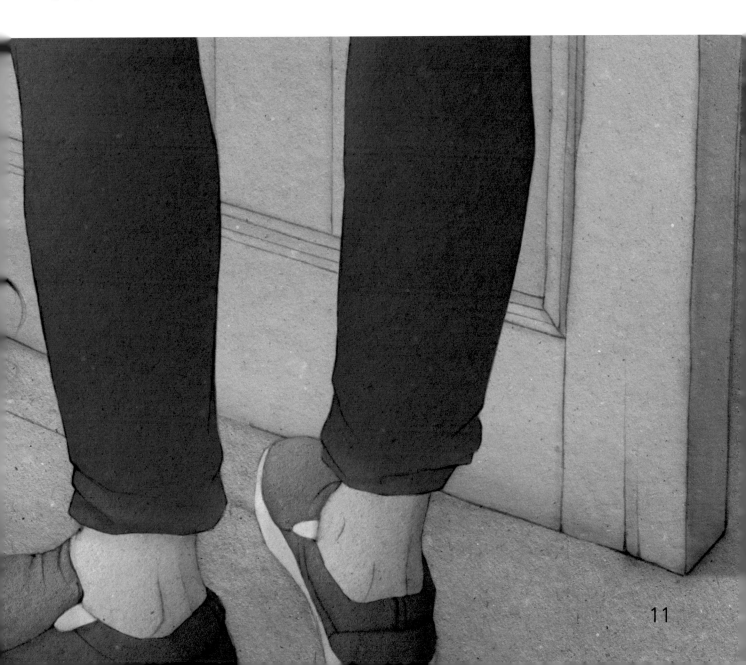

Jazz gets in.

Jazz and Jet nap.

14

After reading

Letters and Sounds: Phase 3

Word count: 40

Focus phonemes: /j/ /w/ /y/ /z/ /qu/ /sh/ /ch/ /th/ zz

Common exception words: by, the

Curriculum links: Understanding the World

Early learning goals: Reading: use phonic knowledge to decode regular words and read them aloud accurately, read some common irregular words

Developing fluency

- Your child may enjoy hearing you read the book.
- Look at page 7 together. Point to the exclamation mark. Ask your child if they know what it is. Explain that we can use exclamation marks to show surprise or excitement. This shows that the text can be read in a particular way, with more expression and enthusiasm.
- Model reading the sentence. Now ask your child to read the sentence with expression.

Phonic practice

- Look at page 2. Ask your child to point to the word, **Jazz**. Together, sound talk and blend it. J/a/zz
- Ask your child if they can find another word with the /z/ sound (page 4 – **zigs**, **zags**). Ask your child to sound talk and blend them.
- Can your child think of any other words with the /z/ sound? (e.g. *zoo*, *zebra*)
- Now look at "I spy sounds" on pages 14 to 15. How many words can your child spot that have the /z/ sound in them (*buzz*, *zebra*, *fizzy*) or the /y/ sound in them (*yellow*, *yelling*)?

Extending vocabulary

- Read each of the words in the list on the left to your child, one at a time, and then read the list on the right. Can they find each word's antonym (opposite) in the list on the right?

quick	(*slow*)	awake
wet	(*dry*)	slow
asleep	(*awake*)	hot
cold	(*hot*)	dry